CREEPY MONSTERS, SLEEPY MONSTERS

a lullaby

JANE YOLEN

illustrated by KELLY MURPHY

WALKER BOOKS
AND SUBSIDIARIES
LONDON · BOSTON · SYDNEY · AUCKLAND

First published 2011 by Walker Books Ltd
87 Vauxhall Walk, London SE11 5HJ

2 4 6 8 10 9 7 5 3 1

Text © 2011 Jane Yolen
Illustrations © 2011 Kelly Murphy

The right of Jane Yolen and Kelly Murphy to be identified as author and illustrator respectively of this work
has been asserted by them in accordance with the Copyright, Designs and Patents Act 1988

This book has been typeset in Wilke Bold

Printed in China

British Library Cataloguing in Publication Data:
a catalogue record for this book is available from the British Library

ISBN 978-1-4063-3170-7

www.walker.co.uk

For Susannah Richards,
who is neither creepy nor a monster
J. Y.

For Natalie, Brendan, Meredith and Scott,
the Fairbanks monsters
K. M.

Monsters creep,
Monsters crawl,

Over the meadow

And up the wall.

Monsters skip-hop,
Monsters tumble.

Monsters slither,
Monsters wave,

All in a hurry
To get to their cave ...

Where monsters grab
A bite to eat,

Then into the bath
To wash their feet.

Then monster prayers,

And into bed ...

But they toss and turn
And bounce instead.

GROWL

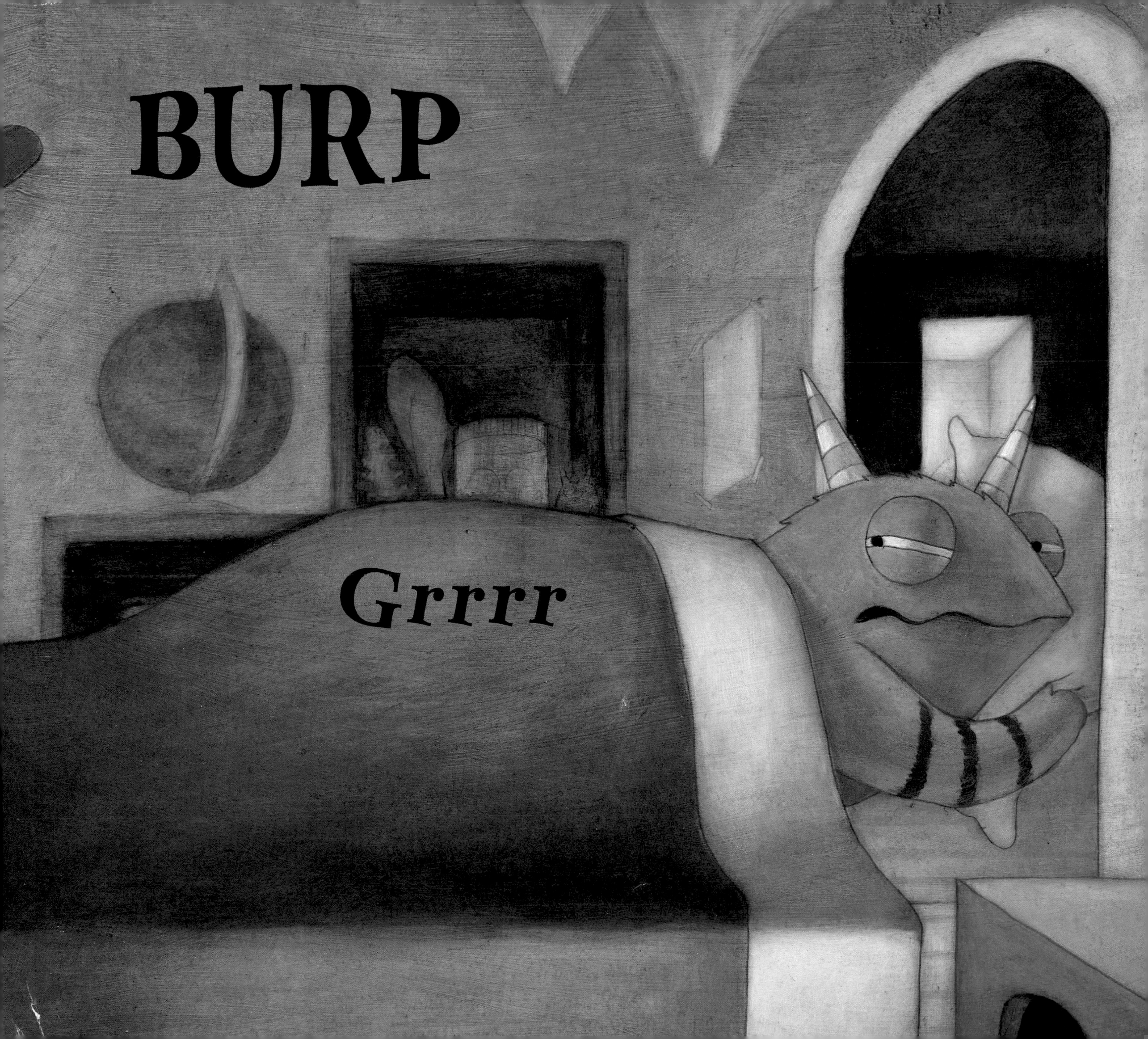
BURP
Grrrr

SNARL

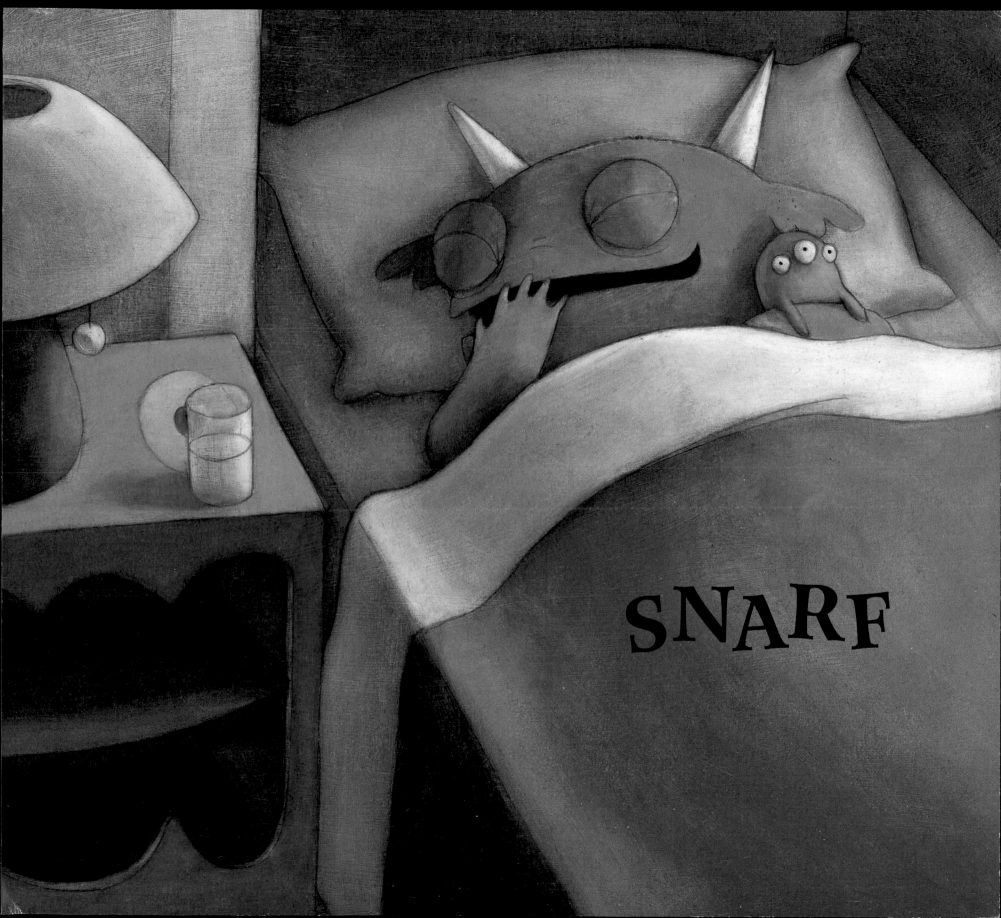